ER
Rau
Rau, Dana Meachen, 1971-

Lots of balloons /

9-15-09

LOTS OF BALLOONS

Written by Dana Meachen Rau
Illustrated by Jayoung Cho

Reading Advisers:

Gale Saunders-Smith, Ph.D., Reading Specialist

*Dr. Linda D. Labbo, Department of Reading Education,
College of Education, The University of Georgia*

LEVEL A

**A COMPASS POINT
EARLY READER**

For Aunt Kate

A Note to Parents

As you share this book with your child, you are showing your new reader what reading looks like and sounds like. You can read to your child anywhere—in a special area in your home, at the library, on the bus, or in the car. Your child will associate reading with the pleasure of being with you.

This book will introduce your young reader to many of the basic concepts, skills, and vocabulary necessary for successful reading. Talk through the details in each picture before you read. Then read the book to your child. As you read, point to each word, stopping to talk about what the words mean and the pictures show. Your child will begin to link the sounds of the letters with the look of the words that you and he or she read.

After your child is familiar with the story, let him or her read the story alone. Be careful to let the young reader make mistakes and correct them on his or her own. Be sure to praise the young reader's abilities. And, above all, have fun.

Gail Saunders-Smith, Ph.D.
Reading Specialist

Compass Point Books
3722 West 50th Street, #115
Minneapolis, MN 55410

Visit Compass Point Books on the Internet at *www.compasspointbooks.com* or e-mail your request to *custserv@compasspointbooks.com*

Library of Congress Cataloging-in-Publication Data

Rau, Dana Meachen, 1971–
   Lots of balloons / written by Dana Meachen Rau ; illustrated by Jayoung Cho.
     p. cm. — (A Compass Point early reader)
   Summary: A child buys different colored balloons to brighten the lives of others.
   ISBN 0-7565-0117-2 (hardcover : library binding)
   [1. Balloons—Fiction. 2. Color—Fiction.] I. Cho, Jayoung, ill. II. Title. III. Series.
PZ7.R193975 Lo 2001
[E]—dc21   2001001597

"May I have a balloon . . .

s Balloon

3

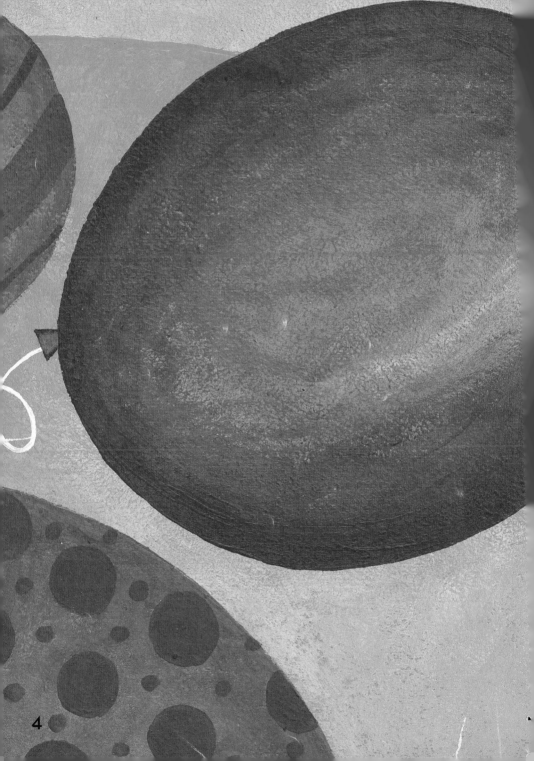

as red as an apple?"

"Here you go."

"May I have a balloon
as blue as the sky?"

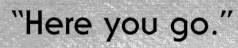

"Here you go."

11

"May I have a balloon
as green as the grass?"

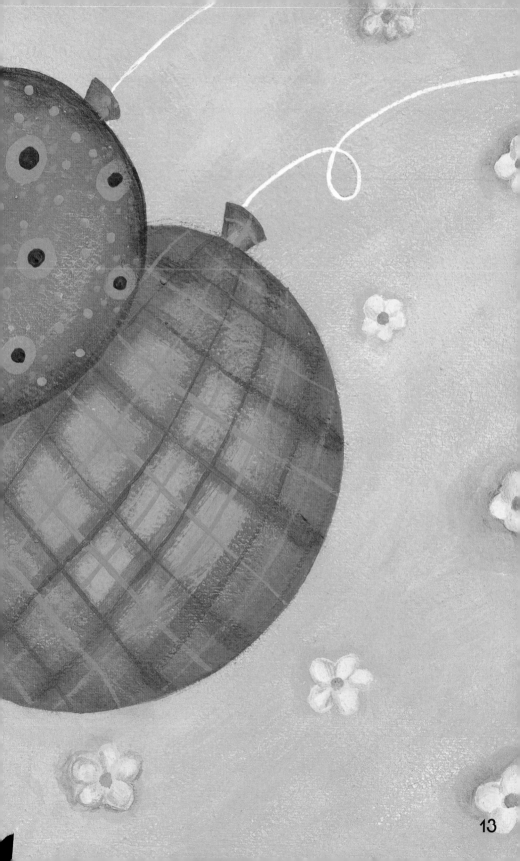

"Here you go."

"May I have a balloon
as yellow as the sun?"

17

"Here you go."

18

19

"May I have all of your
balloons?"

"Now I have no more balloons!"

"There are lots of balloons
for everyone!"

23

Word List

(In this book: 31 words)

a	go	of
all	grass	red
an	green	sky
apple	have	sun
are	here	the
as	I	there
balloon	lots	yellow
balloons	may	you
blue	more	your
everyone	no	
for	now	

About the Author

Dana Meachen Rau's favorite color is blue. She wears blue clothes, drives a blue car, sleeps with a blue blanket, and lives in a house with blue walls. She also loves balloons and sometimes ties them to the back of the chairs in the dining room, even when it isn't anyone's birthday. She lives with her husband, Chris, and son, Charlie, in Farmington, Connecticut, where she has written more than fifty books for children.

About the Illustrator

As a mother of a little girl, Joowon, Jayoung Cho likes to decorate parties with lots of balloons. Ms. Cho is a graduate of the University of Arizona, where she received a master of fine arts degree. Her graduate work has been included in the collections of the Children's Museum of Indianapolis. This is her first picture book.